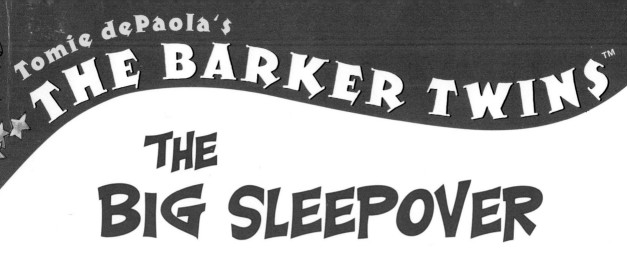

Tomie dePaola's
THE BARKER TWINS™

THE
BIG SLEEPOVER

written by Gail Herman
illustrated by Emilie Kong

based on the Barker Twins characters
created by Tomie dePaola

Grosset & Dunlap • New York

© 2004 by Tomie dePaola. All rights reserved. Published by Grosset & Dunlap, a division of Penguin Young Readers Group, 345 Hudson Street, New York, New York 10014. THE BARKER TWINS and GROSSET & DUNLAP are trademarks of Penguin Group (USA) Inc. Printed in the U.S.A.

Library of Congress Cataloging-in-Publication Data

Herman, Gail, 1959–
The big sleepover / written by Gail Herman ; illustrated by Emilie Kong ;
based on the Barker Twins characters created by Tomie dePaola.
p. cm.—(The Barker twins)
Summary: Moffie is used to doing everything first, but when her twin,
Morgie, gets invited to a sleepover first, she becomes jealous, and also realizes that they have never spent the night apart.
ISBN 0-448-43482-2 (pbk.)
[1. Sleepovers—Fiction. 2. Separation anxiety—Fiction. 3. Behavior—Fiction. 4. Twins—Fiction. 5. Dogs—Fiction.]
I. Kong, Emilie, ill. II. De Paola, Tomie. III. Title. IV. Series.
PZ7.H4315Big 2004
[E]—dc22

2004001045

ISBN 0-448-43482-2   10 9 8 7 6 5 4 3 2 1

Moffie and Morgie were twins. They were born on the same day of the same afternoon, at almost the same time. But Moffie was born first.

Moffie was the first to walk, and the first to bark. Morgie didn't mind.

I do everything first, Moffie thought. *That's just the way it is.*

One day, Morgie and Moffie were playing school with Marcos. He was their new adopted little brother. Moffie was the teacher. The phone rang and Mama called to Morgie, "It's Billy."

When Morgie came back, he was very excited. "Guess what?" he said. "Billy invited me to his house later."

Moffie said, "So what? What's so exciting about that?"
Morgie went to Billy's house lots of times.

"It's for a sleepover!" Morgie said as they all went downstairs for a snack.

A sleepover! Moffie tried to smile.

"So what?" she said again. "I've been on a sleepover. Remember? Marcos and I slept in your room. We made a tent." But Moffie knew that didn't really count.

"You come back soon?" Marcos asked.

"*Sí*, Marcos. Yes. I will be back tomorrow morning."

Moffie wanted to forget about Morgie's sleepover. His room was next to hers. Every night just before they went to sleep, they knocked on the wall to each other. Two times. It meant, "Sweet dreams."

"Come on," Moffie said. "Let's go back and play school some more."

"I can't!" Morgie said. "I have to go pack."

"Fine!" said Moffie angrily as she followed Morgie into his room. "We'll just play without you."

Morgie got out four books, some Mighty Mutt action figures, his bat and baseball glove, all his favorite T-shirts, and his dinosaur pajamas. And, of course, he also packed T-Rex and Steggie so he and Billy could play dinosaur attack.

"It's going to be fun!" Morgie said. "Billy has a bunk bed. I get to sleep on top. And his mom says she'll let us watch a movie after dinner."

"Are you sure you want to go?" Moffie asked.

"What if you fall off the bed?" Moffie went on. "And Mama's making macaroni and cheese tonight. Our favorite."

Morgie frowned. "Uh, sure . . . I'm sure I want to go." But he didn't sound so sure.

But he stuffed his old blanket in his bag, just in case he got homesick.

Then he reached for the checkers game. He and Moffie loved checkers. They played almost every night.

"You can't take that!"
Moffie said.
  "Can too!"
  "Can not!"
  "Can too! I want to teach
Billy to play. I'll bring it
back!"

"Here! Just take it!" Moffie cried.
"I can't wait for you to leave!"

She let go of the box.
The checkers went flying.

"Come on!" Morgie said. "Help me pick them up!"

"No!" Moffie marched out of Morgie's room.

If Morgie was going to Billy's, Moffie wanted a friend to sleep over. Mama said that was fine. Now Moffie would be the first one to have a friend sleep over at their house. *So there, Morgie*, she thought. When Sally said yes, Moffie jumped up and down. She ran to tell Marcos.

"Guess what! Sally's coming to stay over," Moffie told Marcos. "We'll play with you tonight. You won't miss Morgie at all."
"Marcos head hurts. Marcos tired."

All afternoon, Moffie stayed in her room. Morgie stayed in his room.

Marcos stayed in his room. He didn't feel well.

Moffie did not even say good-bye when Morgie left with Papa.

Later, the telephone rang. It was Sally.
"Sally can't come," Moffie told Mama.
"Well, we'll invite her another time."
"Hey!" said Moffie. "I can read to Marcos."

"I'm sorry," Mama said to Moffie. "Marcos has a cold. I don't want you to catch it. And he needs to get some sleep."

The house was so quiet. No Marcos. No Morgie.

But Mama and Papa were home. And Moffie had them all to herself. After dinner, they played Old Maid.

Then they baked cookies. Moffie stirred and mixed. But Morgie
wasn't there to take turns. It was fun, but it wasn't as much fun.

When she was brushing her teeth, Moffie thought about how Morgie liked to gargle really loud. Just to make her laugh.
"You know what? I miss Morgie." Moffie sighed. "Can I call him?"

"Hello, Morgie," Moffie said. "I'm sorry we had a fight and that I was mean. I miss you."

"Moffie!" Morgie said. "I was just going to call you. I miss you too."

"And do you know what?" Morgie went on. "Billy wants you to come for breakfast tomorrow. His mom is making chocolate chip pancakes."

"I'll be there!" Moffie said. "And don't forget to knock good night."

Moffie didn't forget. And neither did Morgie.